DISNEY's

Beauty and the BEAST

ADAPTED BY CATHERINE MCCAFFERTY

*This is the story of Belle and how she came to love the lonely Beast.
Read along with me as we embark on an exciting adventure. You
will know it is time to turn the page when you hear this sound...
Just follow along, and enjoy this wonderful tale about Belle, the
Beast, and all of their friends!*

Story Reader

One cold, stormy night, an old woman begged at a prince's door. She offered the prince a rose, but the selfish prince would not let her stay at his castle. The beggar, who was really quite

magical, changed into a beautiful woman, much to the prince's surprise. Then she cast a spell on the prince, turning him into an ugly beast. Only if he could learn to love, and earn the love of another, could he become human again.

Beyond the woods of the Beast's castle lived a young woman named Belle. Belle loved books. Everyone in the village wondered why Belle did not like the handsome villager Gaston.

Gaston planned to marry Belle, whether she liked him or not.

"She's the most beautiful girl in town," he boasted. "That makes her the best. And don't I deserve the best?"

If the villagers thought that Belle was odd, they thought her father, Maurice, was even odder. Maurice liked to invent things. That very day, he had finished his newest invention: a machine that chopped wood by itself.

"You are sure to win first prize at the fair tomorrow, Papa!" said Belle. "Good-bye! Good luck!"

Deep in the forest, wolves frightened Maurice's horse, Phillipe, and he ran off, leaving Maurice alone. Maurice found his way to the Beast's dark castle. Maurice was greeted by an enchanted clock named Cogsworth and a candelabra named Lumiere. The spell that

had turned the Prince into the Beast had also turned his servants into household objects! The Beast soon discovered Maurice, and made him a prisoner in his castle.

When Phillipe returned alone, Belle knew
that her father was in trouble. She asked
Phillipe to lead her to the dark castle to find her
father.

"What is this place?" Belle whispered as she
walked the dim hallway. "Papa?" She called
out.

Maurice heard her—but so did the Beast!

"He's my prisoner!" the Beast roared when Belle asked him to free her father.

"If I take his place, will you let him go?" Belle offered.

"Yes," said the Beast, "but you must promise to stay here forever."

Belle tried not to think of the Beast's fangs and claws. "You have my word," she promised.

One day, Belle wandered into the West Wing—the only place in the castle the Beast had forbidden her to go. There, she found the magic rose that had been enchanted on the night that the Prince became the Beast. Belle did not know that the Beast had to learn—and earn—love before its last petal fell or he would remain a beast forever.

Suddenly the Beast appeared behind her!

"Get out!" he roared at Belle. He was afraid she would touch the rose.

In time, the Beast learned from Belle's kindness. An
Belle began to see a true beauty within the Beast. Whe
Belle said that she missed her father, the Beast gave her
an enchanted mirror to see Maurice.

And when Belle saw that her father was sick, the Be
said, "You must go to him. I release you." His last hop
for love left with Belle.

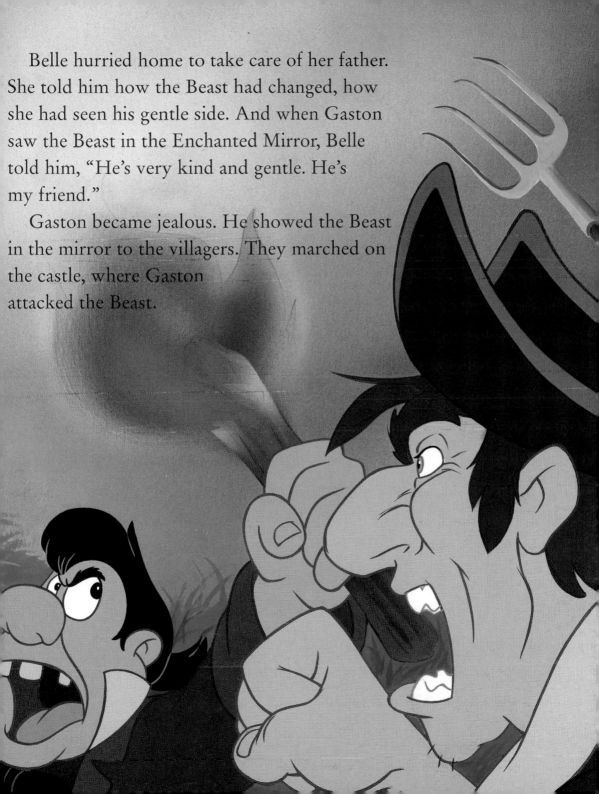

Belle hurried home to take care of her father.
She told him how the Beast had changed, how
she had seen his gentle side. And when Gaston
saw the Beast in the Enchanted Mirror, Belle
told him, "He's very kind and gentle. He's
my friend."

Gaston became jealous. He showed the Beast
in the mirror to the villagers. They marched on
the castle, where Gaston
attacked the Beast.

Belle raced to the Beast's side and found him badly hurt. Deep within the castle, the last petal began to fall from the enchanted rose.

"Please don't leave me," Belle sobbed. "I love you!" Through her tears, Belle saw a magical light touch the Beast.

The spell was broken! The Beast became the prince he had once been—but now he had kindness in his heart, and was beautiful both inside and out.

For the rest of their lives, the prince and Belle shared the beauty of their love and lived happily ever after.